Little Naughty Duck

Marilyn Bradford

Print information available on the last page

Rev. date: 11/20/2015

To order additional copies of this book, contact:
Xlibris
1-888-795-4274
www.Xlibris.com
Orders@Xlibris.com

ACKNOWLEDGEMENTS

Rian Hollowell, my granddaughter, thanks, for reading my manuscripts and just being there for Grandmother.

Thank you, Jaden Hollowell, my grandson for downloading my work and showing it to your teacher, and friends. You're the best little promoter.

To my little friend, Dannon Wilson. Enjoy your dog collection.

Thank you, Johnnie Walker, for the wonderful illustrations. They make the story come to life.

Thank you, Jay Salton, for editing.

The sun rose early on Mr. Mackey's farm. Rowdy Rooster, wearing his brightly colored feathers, would jump atop the barnyard fence and crow as loud as he could, "Cock-a-doodle-do!"

When the other animals heard Rowdy Rooster crow, they knew it was time to get up.

Mrs. Hoagie Hog, who wore her black and white pigskin, called to her little piglets, "It's time to go and take our morning mud bath," and off the little piglets would go to bathe in the mud.

Mrs. Henie Hen, who was a Rhode Island Red and known for her brownish red plumage, would fly off her roost and call to her little bitties, "Come my little chicks. It's time to eat breakfast." And off they went.

Mrs. Moody Cow, who had won many blue Ribbons in the county fair, would moo and call her baby calf

"It's time to go and graze in the pasture." and baby calf would follow his mother to pasture.

Mrs. Ducky Duck would ruffle her feathers and quack to her little ducklings,

"Get together my little ducklings, and let's go down to the pond for a morning swim."

All her little ducks would line up and follow Mother Duck to the pond, but Little Duck did not like to listen to his mother. He would always complain.

"I do not want to go to the pond to swim.

Today I will spend the day doing what I want to do," he thought to himself.

So on this day, he did not follow his mother, sisters, and brothers to the pond.

Little Duck decided he would go for a walk and see what there was to see. He had not gone far before a big truck drove by and splashed mud all over him.

"Messy mud," he cried. "Now my feathers are all dirty."

Just as he began to shake the mud from his feathers, some boys saw him.

"Look," the boys yelled, "There is a little duck. Let's get him!"
And the boys started to chase Little Duck. He was so afraid
that he began to run.

He ran into the street and onto a sidewalk café where a lady wearing a big hat was sitting eating her breakfast. When little duck ran under her table, the lady jumped to her feet and began to scream. "There is a duck under my table!"

The waiter ran out of the cafe with a broom. "I will get him," and he too started to chase Little Duck.

Little Duck ran down the street as fast as he could. He ran past a man who was walking a dog. When the dog saw Little Duck, he also began chasing him. Little Duck ran even faster. "Oh," he cried, "I should have stayed home and gone to the pond to swim with my mother."

Then he saw an opening in a fence. He slipped through just in time, but not before the dog snapped off one of his tail feathers.

"Ouch!" he quacked. "That hurt."

He was now tired and hungry. He walked and walked. It was now getting dark and he had no idea where he was. He was afraid and lost. As he walked he saw some big cans sitting behind a store.

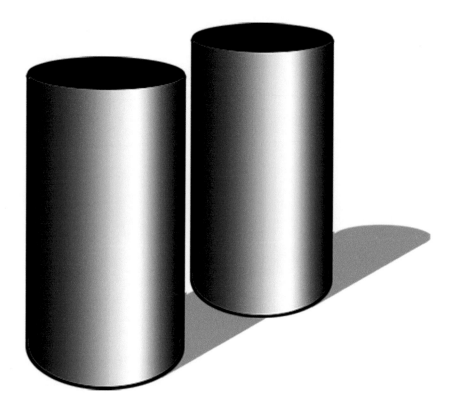

"*Maybe I can rest there,*" he thought. So he nestled down behind the cans and fell asleep at last.

It was just before day break when he was woken by voices. Little Duck peeked out from the can. There before his eyes stood Mr. Mackey, who was delivering tomatoes, corn, and peppers to the storekeeper.

When the two men went inside, Little Duck ran to Mr. Mackey's truck. He jumped up and down flapping his wings, trying to get into the back of the truck.

"If I can get into Mr. Mackey's truck, I shall never say, 'I do not want to go to the pond and swim.'"

All of a sudden, and I do not know how this happened, he flapped his wings as hard as he could. And would you believe this? He jumped into the back of the truck and hid behind some old boxes that sat on the floor.

Soon Mr. Mackey came out of the store. Little Duck could feel the truck moving. After some time the truck stopped. He could see a big sign that read, "Mackey Farm." He was home again. He jumped from the truck and ran as fast as he could. He arrived home just in time to hear his mother say, "Get together my little ducklings, and let's go down to the pond for a morning swim."

"Yes, yes, I will go!" he quacked, and never again did he say,
"I do not want to go to the pond for a swim."

Printed in the United States
by Baker & Taylor Publisher Services